Littlest PetShop

By Maria B. Alfano
Illustrated by Prescott Hill

SCHOLASTIC INC.

New York Toronto London Auckland Sydney

Mexico City New Delhi Hong Kong Buenos Aires

ISBN-13: 978-0-545-07902-0
ISBN-10: 0-545-07902-0

LITTLEST PET SHOP is a trademark of Hasbro and is used with permission.
© 2009 Hasbro. All Rights Reserved.

Published by Scholastic Inc. SCHOLASTIC and associated logos
are trademarks and/or registered trademarks of Scholastic Inc.

12 11 10 9 8 7 6 5 4 3 2 1   9 10 11 12 13/0

Printed in the U.S.A.
First printing, April 2009

DRAW! COLOR! COLLECT!

WELCOME, FRIENDS!

Join the fun as you learn to draw all of your favorite LITTLEST PET SHOP pals. From pandas to puppies, you can create your very own pet shop full of friends!

STEP BY STEP!

The instructions in this book are broken down into small steps. The new lines to draw in each step will show up in a different color, so you'll always know what to draw next.

You will need:
A pencil
Some paper
An eraser

You may also want:
Colored pencils, markers, crayons, watercolors, poster paint, brushes, cut paper, stickers, glitter, glitter pens, gel pens, scrap paper, tracing paper, and a snack!
(Hey, everyone gets hungry!)
Drawing is hard work— but it's also tons of fun!

GETTING STARTED

PICTURE PURR-FECT WARM-UP!

Swing your arms in big circles like a monkey. Then stretch out like a cat. All loosened up? Now practice drawing circles, ovals, curves, swishes, swirls, curls, squiggles, zigzags, and curlicues!

JUST FACE IT! HOW TO DRAW FABULOUS FACES

1) Practice drawing faces with this panda pet. Start with a big shape for the head.

2) Draw a crisscross on the head for the face. The crossed lines show you which way your pet is facing. They also help you to know where to draw the eyes, nose, and mouth.

3) Draw one eye on each side of the up-and-down or vertical line. There is less space for the panda's left eye, so start with a smaller circle.

4) If you draw both eyes on the horizontal line, they'll be even for sure!

5) The nose and mouth always sit just below the horizontal line. The vertical line cuts the nose and mouth in half.

You did it! Great job!

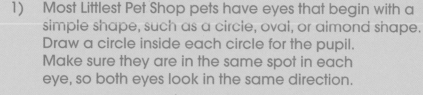
HOW TO DRAW AMAZING EYES

Start out by tracing some of the eyes in this book. You can trace the penguin's eyes on scrap paper a few times before you try to draw them on your own. Tracing isn't cheating–it's a great way to practice!

1) Most Littlest Pet Shop pets have eyes that begin with a simple shape, such as a circle, oval, or almond shape. Draw a circle inside each circle for the pupil. Make sure they are in the same spot in each eye, so both eyes look in the same direction.

2) Now draw the iris using several curved lines around the inside circles.

3) Draw another curved line around the top half of the eye. This will be the eyelid. Next use small curved lines to make eyelashes.

4) Ready to draw highlights? Make a half-moon at the bottom of each eye. Put it in the same spot in each eye.

Congratulations! You just drew excellent penguin eyes! Way to go!

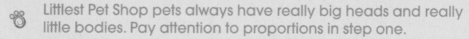

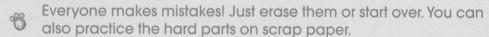

PET TRICKS

Here are some great tips to help you become a terrific Littlest Pet Shop artist:

- Littlest Pet Shop pets always have really big heads and really little bodies. Pay attention to proportions in step one.

- Everyone makes mistakes! Just erase them or start over. You can also practice the hard parts on scrap paper.

- Smudge-proof your drawing. Keep a piece of scrap paper under your hand as you draw.

- Keep your lines light and loose. This makes it easier to erase mistakes. It will also make coloring in your pet easier later on.

- Personalize your pet! Is your pet purple or pink? Does it have long eyelashes or short eyelashes? Once you get the hang of the basics, dress up your pet with your own signature style.

PANDA

Cute and cuddly, this Littlest Pet Shop panda is ready to munch on a bunch of bamboo. Are you ready to make this bear your very first one-of-a-kind drawing? Grab a pencil and get to it!

Step 1

The goal of this step is to get a general sense of the whole pet. Draw a big boxy shape for the head and smaller shapes for the body. Then draw two triangles on top of the head for the ears.

Step 2

Draw simple shapes for the legs, feet, arms, and tail. Then erase any lines you don't need, so your drawing doesn't get too confusing.

Step 3

Look back at pages 4–5 if you need help drawing eyes. Then draw the nose and mouth. Notice how they sit at the very bottom of the face. Add lines to make the ears.

Step 4

Time for details! Start with circles on the bottoms of the panda's paws. Then focus on the eyes. Draw a half circle in each eye to show highlights. Add tiny diamonds to give your panda pizzazz!

Step 5

Make any last-minute changes to your drawing. Then add color! Fill in the lighter areas first—like the pink and lime green. Let them dry. Then add darker colors such as the gray and black on top.

PENGUIN

This friendly penguin wants to be your pal. Whether it's belly-flopping down a snowy hill or waddling in the waves, the penguin is always ready to have fun. Are you ready to have fun with this drawing?

Pet Trick!
Does a step look too hard? Break it down into smaller pieces and practice the steps on scrap paper.

Step 1

Start with a big circle for the head and ovals for the body and flippers. Then use crossed lines to figure out where the face will be.

Step 2

Draw two neat feet! Sketch two small feet at the bottom of the oval you made for the body. Then draw a short curved line between them. Next draw two curves on the body to show off the penguin's belly. Now erase the lines you don't need anymore.

Step 3

Add two curved lines that meet at a point to set the penguin's face. The penguin's eyes are made up of lots of circles. Use the crisscrosses you drew on the face in step 1 to help you keep the eyes even. Don't forget the beak! The penguin needs it to catch fish!

Step 4

Call in the cleanup crew! Erase any extra lines, smudges, or mistakes. Then add details to the eyes, such as eyelids, eyelashes, and half-moons for highlights. Need to make any changes? Make them now.

Step 5

What's black, white, and blue? A penguin drawn by you! Those true-blue penguin eyes are two different shades of turquoise. Remember to color in the black parts last to avoid smudging!

SKUNK

Here's a skunk with spunk! Strolling along with a shy smile, this sweet pet just wants to make friends. Make sure your sweet skunk sketch doesn't stink! Put a piece of scrap paper under your hand as you draw, so you don't smudge the lines.

Step 1

Set the stage with a big boxy head, a tiny body, and a giant swishing tail. Don't worry about how your drawing looks at this stage. Just get down the basics.

Step 2

Draw four legs at the bottom of the body. If you get confused, start with simple triangles. Lift that right front leg to give your skunk dancing feet. Next draw a curved line for the belly. Now draw the signature stripe on the skunk's tail.

Step 3

Check out that curl on the skunk's head! Now draw an upside-down triangle on the forehead. Don't forget the face! Take your time and practice the hard parts on scrap paper if you get stuck.

Step 4

The eyes have it! The details in this drawing are in the eyes. Draw a half-moon at the bottom of each eye. Follow up with a tiny diamond. When you're done, add eyelids and lashes. Then take a good look at your drawing and see if there is anything you want to change.

Step 5

For fun, try drawing the skunk on black paper using a white colored pencil, acrylic paint, or correction fluid pen for the white patches. Your drawing will be unique—just like you!

CAT

Calling all cool cats: Get set to draw this sweet and sassy kitty! This friendly feline is always up for a challenge. Are you ready for your next drawing challenge? Stretch out your drawing hand and get ready to pounce!

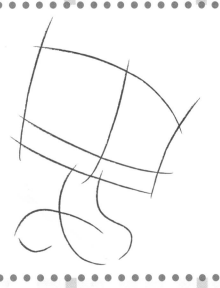

Step 1

Warm up by drawing big swishing lines on scrap paper. Then set up your drawing. The cat's body tilts to the side, so draw a rough rectangle on an angle for the head. Now add a jelly-bean-shaped body. Finish up with two quick curved lines for the tail.

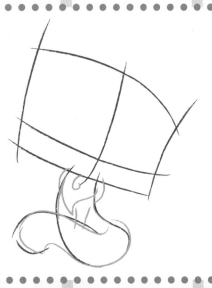

Step 2

Take a closer look at the cat's body. Where is the tail? Where is the leg? Use lots of curved lines to draw them and don't forget to sketch in the patch of fur on the cat's chest.

Step 3

Work on the eyes, then draw a triangle inside a triangle for each ear. The cat's nose is an upside-down triangle. Follow up with an upside-down capital T for a mouth. Then use zigzags to draw the patch of pink on the forehead.

Step 4

You got the basic shape of the eyes down in Step 3. Now it's time to add details. Start by drawing two curved lines at the top of each eye for lids. Then draw a curl in each corner for eyelashes. Add simple lines for eyebrows. Draw purr-fect diamonds and highlights.

Step 5

Steppin' out in stripes! This cat is pretty in pink—right down to the diamonds in her eyes. Here's a tip: Try to keep your pencil lines light as you go along. It will make it easier to color in the lighter shades of pink and blue later on.

Owl

Surprise! Surprise!
All that drawing practice has made you wise!
Now put your hard-earned wisdom to use by
drawing this owl. It'll be a hoot!

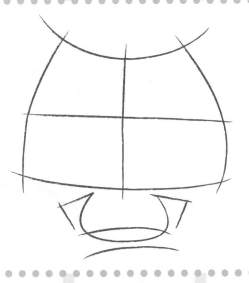

Step 1

Set up your drawing.
This owl's head is
supersized compared to
its body. Draw two curved
lines to show where the
feet will be. Then decide
where you want to draw
the wings and make
your mark.

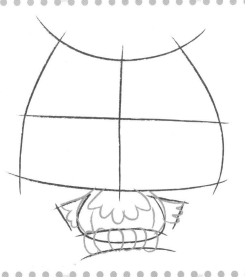

Step 2

C is for claws! This owl
has six of them. Use short
curved lines—kind of
like the letter C—to show
where the talons will go.
Then lightly sketch a few
feathers on the owl's
wings and chest.

Step 3

This owl's eyes are circles inside circles, like most of the Littlest Pet Shop pets. But a simple slanting line at the top of each eye gives them a singular shape. Now take time to draw the ears, beak, and feathers on top of the head.

Step 4

Define those details. Start by drawing two curved lines on the sides of the beak. Then add more feathers to the ears. Take a closer look at the eyes. Are they just the right shape and size? Erase any lines you don't need.

Step 5

Use a bunch of different browns and tans for color. The beak and claws come in two distinct shades of orange. Use the darker shade under the beak to make it look like it's in shadow. Whooo's a drawing star? You are!

SEA HORSE

Whether it's bobbing around out in the sea grass or swimming through the coral reef, this shy sea horse has a special sparkle. Did you know that sea horses turn bright colors when they're having fun with friends? Show off your sketching star power by drawing this sea horse playing with other Littlest Pet Shop pals.

Step 1

Set up for a side view. Start with a big circle for the head. Then draw a curved body. Use a small circle for the tail and a rough rectangle for the snout, or nose. Then draw an upside-down triangle at the top of the head for the coronet.

Step 2

Ready to draw some details on the body? Use three capital U shapes to draw the fin. Next add the curve of the tail. Then do a proportions check. Is the body the right size compared to the head?

Step 3

Erase any lines you don't need. Tweak the shape of the head, snout, and coronet. Then draw the eye. Start with a half-moon instead of a circle this time.

Step 4

Dive into the details! Start by drawing the spines on the sea horse's head and back. They resemble the teeth on a zipper or the edges of a puzzle piece. Work on the eyes and the capital V inside the coronet. Finish up with the stripes on the belly.

Step 5

When coloring the highlight in each eye, first color in the circle with a white colored pencil. Then color in the black, green, and blue sections.

RACCOON

Razzle-dazzle your family and friends with a drawing of this bright-eyed and bushy-tailed raccoon. Don't be afraid to take some drawing risks. If you're too worried about messing up, you may never find out how good you can be!

Step 1

Take a minute to draw the basic shapes of the head and body. Make sure you draw them both on an angle. Use lines to guide you. Then draw a crisscross on the face.

Step 2

Add arms and legs to the raccoon's body. Trace them on scrap paper first if you have a tough time. Tracing is a great way to practice a challenging drawing. Then add a few pointy parts to fluff up the tail.

PUPPY

Bow-wow-wow! You've already finished half of the drawings in this book. Congratulations! Are you ready to tackle a drawing that is doggone cute? This proud puppy is walking on sunshine. With his favorite doggy bone, this playful pup can't help but be happy!

Step 1

Start with a rough sketch. Use a big rectangle for the head, an oval for the body, and triangle shapes for the legs and ears. Take extra time to draw the head on an angle. Notice how that ear swings out to the side.

Step 2

Draw the puppy's body. See how that front leg is up and ready to run? Don't forget the belly and tail!

Step 3

Practice drawing circles on scrap paper before you work on the puppy's eyes. You can even trace around the bottom of a cup, jar, or quarter to help you out. Then add the mouth and clean up the floppy doggy ears.

Step 4

Knickknack, paddy whack, give this dog a bone! Erase the top line of the bone to make it look like it's in the puppy's mouth. Then draw short curved lines on the paws and any other details you need.

Step 5

Color your puppy pal. Try drawing some details of your own. Maybe your puppy carries a ball instead of a bone. Does he wear a collar, a doggy sweater, or even a hat? Try drawing an entire lineup of puppies on parade.

BEE

What's all the buzz about? This cheery bee is flying high. Bee happy with all of your fantastic drawings. You're doing a great job!

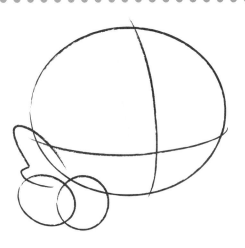

Step 1

Start with a big oval for the head. Then draw a crisscross to set up the face. Add two circles for the body and outline the wing.

Step 2

Make the bee's body look fuzzy by using wavy lines to sketch in the stripes. Now look at all those legs! Can you find places to draw all six of them?

Step 3

Double-check the shape of the head. It might need some fixing up. Then add a big bright smile. Take your time with the eyes. You've had lots of practice!

Step 4

Time for details! Draw the antennae on top of the head and the curlicues on the wings. Erase any lines you don't need and get ready to add color!

Step 5

Yellow is the color of sunshine, and it makes people—and Littlest Pet Shop pets—very happy. So grab your yellow crayon and color away! When you're done, show off your bee-utiful drawing!

HAMSTER

With a sweet smile and its head held high, this happy hamster is ready to make friends. Here's a hamster hint: Practice drawing the hardest parts of this drawing on scrap paper before you add them to your final piece. It will keep you from running in circles later on!

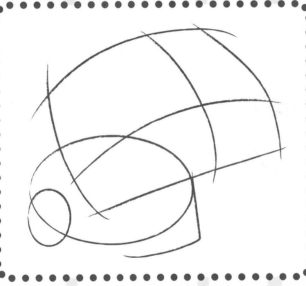

Step 1

The hamster's head is like a rectangle and the body is like an oval. Use this step to get a feel for the entire drawing. Draw lines to show where the feet will go. Keep your lines light and loose.

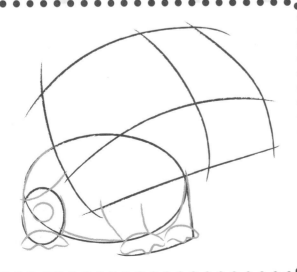

Step 2

Time for a double-check. Did you remember to tilt up the hamster's head in step 1? Great! Now draw the legs and paws. Did you notice that one leg is hiding behind the hamster's body?

Step 3

How eye-catching! The hamster's eyes start with half-moons. Now work on the nose and mouth. The nose sits just above the horizontal line you drew in step 1, and the mouth is right below it. Next add ears and fur to the hamster's head.

Step 4

Step back and take a good look at your drawing. What does it need? Did you draw the curve inside the ear? Draw some more details and fix anything you don't like.

Step 5

Erase any extra lines. Did you add the cute circle patch around the hamster's right eye? Break out the browns! Add touches of purple and pink. Perfect!

LADYBUG

Share the love with this lucky ladybug. But don't bug out! Drawing can be hard, but it's also a ton of fun, especially when you're sketching this bright and cheery ladybug!

Step 1

You know what to do! Start with simple shapes like a big oval head and triangle legs. Use half an oval for the wing. Remember to start simple and save all the hard details for the end.

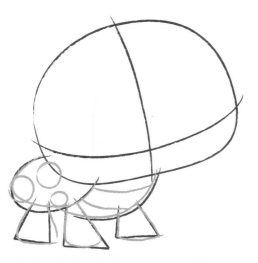

Step 2

Take a minute to shape the body. If you get confused, look at the final drawing to guide you. Then draw curved stripes on the ladybug's belly and circles on the wings.

Step 3

Draw one curve for the top of each eye and one curve for the bottom. Inside each eye, draw a circle. To the right of each circle, draw three curves. Now don't forget to add antennae. Ladybugs need them for touching and smelling.

Step 4

Draw details like the ladybug's fun-loving smile. Then add circular highlights inside the eyes to make them sparkle and shine!

352
2795   Adol. Lit

Step 5

Bright red is the color of energy and confidence. It's the perfect shade to make this lovely ladybug stand out in a crowd!

PEACOCK

Time to strut your stuff! Draw a peacock. They love the spotlight. Just take a look at those fancy tail feathers. Now get ready to show off your sketching skills with this scene-stealing drawing.

Pet Trick!

Keep all of your early drawings. It's fun to see how much better you get.

Step 1

Draw a big shape for the head and a smaller oval for the body. Then add two small triangles for feet. Pick a spot for the tail. Then draw two straight lines topped with a curve.

Step 2

There's a lot to add in this step, so take your time. First connect the shapes you drew in step 1. Next focus on the feet and the peacock's wings. Then fan out those tail feathers with curved lines and ovals.

Step 3

Flip back to pages 4–5 for tips on drawing eyes. When you're done with the eyes, draw two curlicues on top of the head. Then place the beak at the very bottom of the face.

Step 4

Confused about which details to draw first? Start simple. Pick a place to begin, such as the tail. Then add other details bit by bit—like the pattern on the peacock's face and the diamonds in the eyes.

Step 5

Turquoise and lime green are a winning combination! Use a touch of dark blue for the wings and tail feathers. Your drawing will be as pretty as a peacock in no time!

MONKEY

Wow! You're on the last drawing of this book! Here's your chance to monkey around. Experiment with different pens, pencils, and colors. This monkey is happily walking along, but try drawing a monkey hanging from a tree or playing with a friend. Your family and friends will go bananas for your masterpiece!

Step 1

Start this drawing with lots of ovals. Figure out where you want to put the arms and legs and draw rough triangles. Then add a curved line for the tail.

Step 2

Work on the body. Draw paws at the bottom of each arm and leg and put a simple banana in the monkey's paw. Finish the tail.

Step 3

Draw a curl on top of the head. Then draw lots of circles for the eyes. Don't forget other facial features such as the ears, nose, and mouth! Then erase any lines you don't need.

Step 4

Time for details! Finish up the eyes with half-moon highlights. Then draw curved lines inside the ears. Add tiny touches to the nose, mouth, body, and paws. Draw the bow and the banana peel and you're there!

Step 5

You can use the same brown crayons you used to color in the hamster. Use a mellow yellow for the monkey's bow and banana. Don't forget to put a touch of lavender inside each blue eye. Now give yourself a hug! You're done!

YOU DID IT!

A picture is worth a thousand purrs! Now that you can draw so many of your favorite Littlest Pet Shop pets, how are you going to show off your skills?

Here are some fun and fabulous ideas:

- Make gifts for your friends or decorate your diary, schoolbooks, note cards, and postcards.

- Set up a drawing gallery on your refrigerator or in your family room. You can even host an art opening party for your family and friends with juice and mini-sandwiches.

- Draw big versions of each pet on cardboard or thick paper. Cut them out and put on a play or puppet show.

- Now that you're an eye expert, make Littlest Pet Shop pet masks. Just draw the head on a paper plate and cut out a small hole in each eye so you can see!

- Scan your drawing into the computer, change the colors, and print out tons of party invitations, or even create your own Littlest Pet Shop e-cards.

- Host a Littlest Pet Shop Drawing Party with your friends!

Now that you've had tons of practice, try creating all-new pets. Start your very own unique collection of fabulous Littlest Pet Shop pets!